BENJAMIN'S SLING

Eileen M. Berry

Photography by Craig Oesterling

journeyforth®

Greenville, South Carolina

Bethlehem Manger

This first-century limestone feeding trough, or manger, comes from Bethlehem, the birthplace of Christ. Dr. and Mrs. Frank Bowen were called to the Church of the Nativity in 1937 by a priest from a Greek Orthodox church; evidently a workman had broken through a wall in the church and discovered the manger among other things. Dr. and Mrs. Bowen purchased the manger in 1938 from the Church of the Nativity, which is believed to be built over the place where Christ was born.

While Bob Jones University Museum & Gallery does not and cannot claim that this manger is the one in which the newborn Christ was laid, it is typical of the stone mangers cut from the caves in Bethlehem at the time of Christ's birth. Its simplicity and crudeness illustrate life at the time of His birth; He was born in the humblest and lowliest circumstances among the poor of the Jewish people.

Bethlehem Manger, 1st century

From the Bowen Collection of Antiquities at Bob Jones University Museum & Gallery, Greenville, SC

And so it was, that, while they were there, the days were accomplished that she should be delivered. And she brought forth her firstborn son, and wrapped him in swaddling clothes, and laid him in a manger; because there was no room for them in the inn.

Luke 2:6–7

Benjamin's Sling
Written by Eileen M. Berry
Photography and design by Craig Oesterling
© 2010 by BJU Press
Greenville, SC 29614
JourneyForth Books is a division of BJU Press

Printed in the United States of America
ISBN 978–1–60682–064–3
15 14 13 12 11 10 9 8 7 6 5 4 3 2 1

To Rhonda,
twice-born sister,
forever friend

Benjamin lies with his head
pillowed on his rolled-up cloak,
looking up at the stars,
one hand resting on Yedi.
Five months now,
since the night his father died,
his pet lamb has slept near him.
Twining his fingers into the soft wool,
he feels the gentle rise and fall of her side.

Yedi sleeps, but Benjamin cannot.

He turns on his side,
sees the lights of Bethlehem
at the foot of the quiet hillside.
He raises himself for a better view.
City lights make him think of homes,
of warm beds indoors,
of families together.
He stares at the lights
until his eyesight blurs.

Then he turns his face up
to the colder, lonelier lights—
a solemn white moon
and pale, distant stars.
A sudden shadow
falling across his face
makes Benjamin jump.

His hand burrows for the sling
hidden beneath his cloak.
Always now he clutches the sling
when startled in the night.

Just above his head, Caleb's voice speaks.
"Still awake, Benjamin?"

"Caleb, you scared me."
Benjamin stuffs the sling
beneath his cloak again.

He looks up
into the older shepherd's face,
fear seeping away.

"You must sleep, Benjamin.
It is not your turn to keep watch tonight."

Benjamin sits all the way up.
Yedi rouses herself, lifts her head,
nuzzles Benjamin's hand,
stretches out to sleep again.

"I was thinking of Father.
It was a night like this.
So quiet
when those . . . wolves came."

Caleb only waits, silent.

"I wanted to help Father,
but I was so afraid.
I couldn't move,
couldn't see what was happening,
just heard snarling and shouting
and then the wolves were gone."

Can Caleb see what a coward I am?

Finally Caleb speaks.
"I was thinking of your father too.
He died nobly, Benjamin.
He died protecting his flock.
A good shepherd risks
everything
for his sheep."

Benjamin says nothing.
A shepherd dying
so that sheep can live?
It seems wrong.

"Your father loved you, my boy.
Son of my right hand he called you.
After your mother died,
you were the apple of his eye.
Would have fought
ten times as many wild beasts

barehanded
to protect you.
What a brave man he was."

"I wish I could be like Father."

Benjamin pulls out his sling
and drapes it around his wrist.
Even in the dark, he can see its beauty—
woven of sheep's wool,
black and white strands.

"Father made this sling for me—
and taught me how to use it.
I carry it with me
everywhere.
As long as I have it,
I will be safe."

Benjamin moves his arm in short, tight circles,
twirling the sling
faster,
faster,
a whirling, whirring thing.

If only he could spin away his fears.
He isn't sure what he'll do
if the wolves come back.
He's so unlike his father,
so terribly afraid
of shadows,
of howling in the night,
of losing someone else he loves.

He drops his arm.
The sling slaps against his wrist.

"May I remind you of something?"
Caleb's voice is quiet.

Benjamin looks up,
liking the way Caleb treats him
like a grown man.
"Of course."

Caleb softly begins to sing.
"Though I walk the lonely valley
With death's shadow ever near,
Still the Lord my Shepherd leads me,
And no evil will I fear.

"Do you know who wrote that psalm, Benjamin?"

"David."
His favorite story—
a shepherd boy who kills a giant
with only a sling.

Caleb gently takes the sling
from Benjamin.

"Yes, it was David.
A shepherd boy who trusted Yahweh.

A king who trusted Yahweh.
In trusting he found strength
to be brave.

"Yahweh is the One we must trust
in any danger, my boy—
not a person,
not a weapon,
not anything else.
We must trust Him alone."

"But Yahweh doesn't always . . ."
Benjamin stops,
presses his lips tightly together.

Caleb fingers the sling,
tracing its fine weave.

"I do not understand His ways, Benjamin.
He acts with a skill
we cannot always see
till later.
But do not fear.
David trusted Him
to the end of his life
and found Him good.

"You and I must do the same."

He hands the sling back to Benjamin.

Benjamin stares past Caleb
at the lights of Bethlehem.

Lying down he pulls up his blanket
till the scratchy wool
brushes his chin.
He stuffs his sling under his cloak again.

Maybe David trusted Yahweh
a little.
But David also had a sling.
That was what killed the giant.
Yedi stirs.
Benjamin snuggles closer to her warmth,
closes his eyes.
Caleb's hand rests a moment on his head.
Then the grass rustles
as his friend walks away.

Benjamin is suddenly wide awake.
It is not morning,
but the hillside is flooded in brilliant light.
A very white light,
the whitest he has ever seen.
Benjamin's heart pounds.

He clutches his sling and gropes
for one of the stones he keeps close by.

Around him sheep raise their heads.
Shepherds stand outlined
against the light.
Fretful bleating
and tense voices
echo up and down the hillside.

Benjamin squints into the brightness.
Someone is standing
in the center of the light.
A blazingly bright form,
maybe a man.
A voice thunders.
"Fear not!"

Nearby a shepherd murmurs one word—
"Angel."
Silence settles on the hill.

"Fear not."
This time Benjamin catches
a note of joy in the voice.
The pounding of his heart slows.

"I bring you good tidings
of great joy,
which shall be to all people.
For unto you is born
this day in the city of David
a Saviour, which is Christ the Lord."

Benjamin loosens his grip on the sling,
and it slips to the ground.
The joy in the angel's voice
is reaching out to him,

circling him,
drawing him into the light.

But what is the angel saying now?
They will find a baby
wrapped in cloths,
lying in a manger.

A manger.
A baby lying
in a feeding trough?
What can it mean?

Suddenly
a great crowd of angels joins the one.
Joyful voices explode into song.

Glory to God in the highest,
and on earth peace, good will toward men.
The singing ends.
The angels disappear.
A hush hangs over the shepherds.

Then all begin speaking at once.

"We must go now and see the Christ!"
"Is this the Promised One?"
"Who else could it be?
The angel said it was a Savior,
the Lord Himself!"

"We must search the city of David."
"Yes, let's go to Bethlehem!"

Caleb is beside Benjamin,
his hand on the boy's shoulder.
"Stay with me.
We will all go together."

"But, Caleb—the sheep?"

Caleb's face crinkles
into the smile
that Benjamin loves.

"The Lord told us to go, my boy.
He will take care of our sheep."

Benjamin glances over his shoulder at Yedi.
She watches him, bleats.
In his mind Benjamin hears
the snarling of wolves again.

Benjamin takes a few steps toward the lamb.

Caleb's voice
stops him gently.
"Benjamin, we must do
as the angel of the Lord said.
Remember, my boy.
Who is the One we must trust?"

Benjamin does not answer.
He bites his trembling lip,

turns,
follows the men who have begun to run.
His thoughts whirl, swift as a sling.
He thinks of Yedi,
unprotected on the hillside,
thinks of the wolves,
thinks of his father,
thinks of the baby.
Sometimes he thinks he can hear
the angel's song
lingering on the wind.
In his mind he sings it
to the rhythm of his pounding feet.

Glory to God!
And on earth peace . . .

In the darkest part of the night
they enter a small shelter,
dim with rough-hewn walls like a cave.
Lamplight flickers
on two young faces—a man's and a woman's.
Sitting on the floor of the cave,
they watch a baby
sleeping in the stone manger
between them.

They look up without surprise.

"Welcome," says the man.
"I am Joseph.
This is my wife, Mary."

Benjamin stares at the baby.
He is completely still,
his tiny face calm and happy
as if enjoying pleasant dreams.
That's the way I'd like to sleep.

"And the baby's name?" asks a shepherd.

"His name is Jesus."

Caleb is the first
to fall on his knees.
"*Jesus*.
It means 'Yahweh saves.' "

One by one, the other shepherds kneel
around the manger.

Benjamin alone hangs back,
watching from the doorway.

Mary's eyes
are large with wonder.
"It is true," Joseph says.
"You have found the Savior,
Christ, the Lord."

Caleb's gaze roves among the shepherds,
comes to rest on Benjamin.
"Come closer, lad."

Slowly Benjamin moves from the doorway.

On the wall behind Mary,
a shadow looms,
a giant head with curved horns.
Fear surges through him.
He plunges his hand
into the pouch of his cloak.

The pouch is empty.

In that moment
he remembers his sling—
left back on the grassy hill.

The shadow dips and rises
as the ox in the darkened corner stall
swings its head.
Benjamin hesitates,
uncertain.

Still the baby is before him,
sleeping in perfect peace,
little face untouched by shadows.

How can Someone so small
make me feel so safe?
Safer than I ever felt with my sling.

Caleb smiles,
lays his large hand
on the baby's head.
He stretches the other hand out to Benjamin.
"You need not be afraid, my boy.
This is the Promised One
that David looked for,
that your own father waited for.
Now in your lifetime,
He is here.
Come to the Savior."

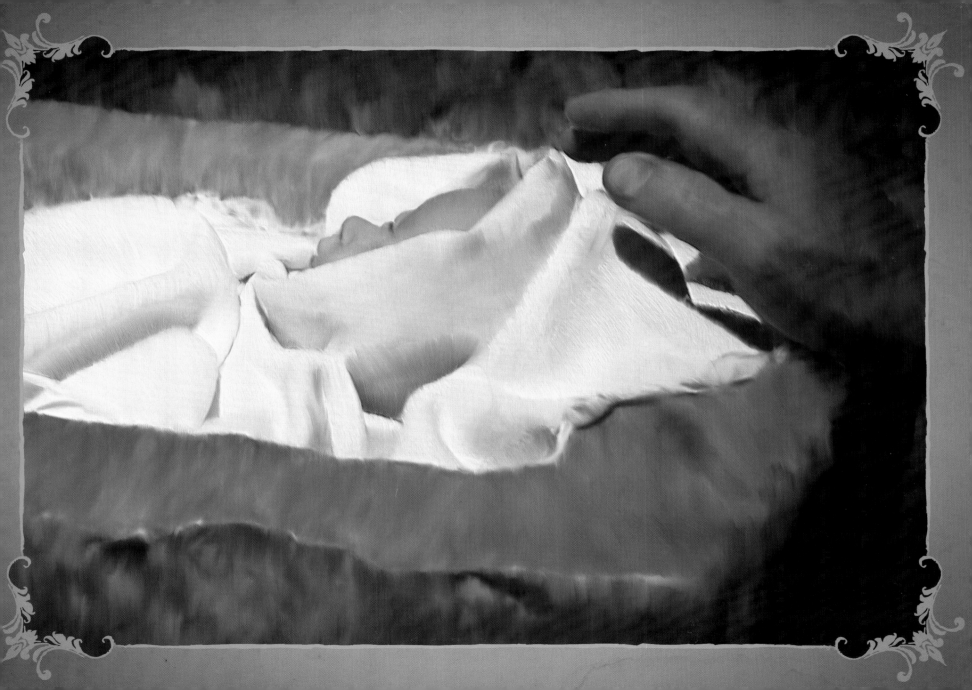

Benjamin fixes his eyes
on the baby's face.
The Savior.
My Savior.
Isn't that what the angel said?
"Born for you."

Benjamin drops to his knees.
He edges closer
and closer.

Close enough to lay his hand
on the cool stone manger.
Close enough to brush the trough
where the baby nestles.
Close enough to rest a finger
on the rough cloths
wrapping the tiny body.

This Jesus is the One
David trusted,
the One
my father trusted,
and the One
Caleb trusts.
He gazes into the baby's face.

And the One I will trust—
from this moment on.